Verity Fairy
and
Sleeping Beauty

Contents

Fairy Tale Kingdom … 4

1   Verity Plans a Party … 6

2   Gifts from the Fairies … 16

3   Nissa's Curse … 24

4   A Marshmallow … 30

5	A Fourth Birthday	**36**
6	The Prince's Castle	**42**
7	Three Sparkly Stars	**50**
	Fairy Quiz	**62**
	Acknowledgements	**64**

Fairy Tale Kingdom

Rapunzel's Tower

Cinderella's House

Enchanted Tree

Fairy Godmother's House

Prince Charming's Castle

Seven Dwarfs' House

- Sleeping Beauty's Castle
- Clock Tower
- Celeste's House
- Verity's House
- Wicked Queen's Castle

Chapter One
Verity Plans a Party

At the bottom of the enchanted tree was a little wooden door. It was framed with pretty snowdrops and hidden by golden leaves. This was where Tatiana, the Queen of the Fairies, lived. One chilly evening, Verity followed Tatiana through the door, in a hurry to escape the cold. She waited patiently next to the blazing fire to be given her next task.

Tatiana removed her long golden cloak and sat down at her desk opposite Verity.

Verity was very excited. Each month Tatiana gave the fairies tasks to complete. If they did well, they were rewarded with a beautiful sparkly star. Verity really wanted to be the first fairy to earn a rare lilac star. This could be her chance!

"Verity, I have some exciting news."

Tatiana clasped her hands together. "The King and Queen are throwing a party to welcome their baby daughter to the kingdom. The fairies will all present their special gifts. And they would like you to organize it!"

"Ooh, that is exciting!" Verity hopped from one foot to the other. Her purple boots sparkled. "I LOVE parties! Can I choose the cake? I know exactly which cake to have... a marshmallow one."

"Yes, I suppose so," laughed Tatiana.

"It's important that all the fairies meet the new princess and enjoy this magnificent party."

But Verity was busy thinking of the cake. Marshmallows were her favourite sweet and she had always wanted a marshmallow cake.

"Verity, are you listening?" Tatiana raised an eyebrow.

"Oh, yes," replied Verity confidently. "Don't worry, just leave everything to me. This is going to be the best party ever!"

As Verity arrived back at her house, she saw her best friend, Celeste. The two fairies loved spending time together. They liked baking cakes, playing football, practising **dance routines,** and making necklaces from buttercups. They also loved reading.

---

dance routines   Set pattern of steps in a particular order

"Look what I've got!" Celeste sang happily. "The new copy of *Sparkle Time*." This was their favourite magazine. They waited eagerly each week for the new copy to arrive in the shop.

"I'm sorry, Celeste," said Verity proudly, "but I can't read *Sparkle Time* with you today. I am organizing a party to welcome the new baby princess."

Celeste clapped her hands together excitedly. "Ooh Verity, that's great! Can I help?"

Verity smoothed down her rainbow-coloured skirt. She **swayed** from side to side while she pretended to think. "Of course you can," she giggled. "You can help me think of who we should invite."

---

swayed   Swung

The two fairies ran inside Verity's pretty thatched-roof house. They hurried through the little green front door and into the kitchen. A small circular table stood in the middle with two wooden chairs.

"OK, let's make a list!" said Verity. She grabbed a piece of paper and a pencil.

Celeste said all the names of the fairies aloud as Verity wrote them down. "Well, there's Fay, Fleur, Willow, and Dawn... Then Astor, Sky, Lila, Tatiana, Nissa, and me and you."

Verity opened the drawer in the dresser next to the table. She handed Celeste a pile of glittery invitations and two gold-ink pens.

"Wow, these are amazing invitations!" Celeste opened her eyes wide with excitement. "Shall we write them now?"

"Yes, and then we can deliver them." Verity lightly clapped her hands together. "This is going to be the best party!" Verity frowned as she looked at Celeste's list again. "I'm not inviting Nissa," she said, shaking her head.

The week before, Verity had invited all her fairy friends over for a picnic. She had tried really hard to make it special. There had been lots of fun games and delicious food. But Nissa had spent the whole afternoon being grumpy and had barely spoken to anyone. It still upset Verity to think about it.

"Really? I'm not sure you should leave her out." Celeste suddenly looked very worried.

"I don't want Nissa to spoil the party for the princess," Verity said firmly.

"I think it would be better to invite her," said Celeste kindly. "You might accidentally tell her about the party and this would upset her." Celeste knew that sometimes Verity blurted out the truth. This often got her into trouble.

But Verity had made up her mind.

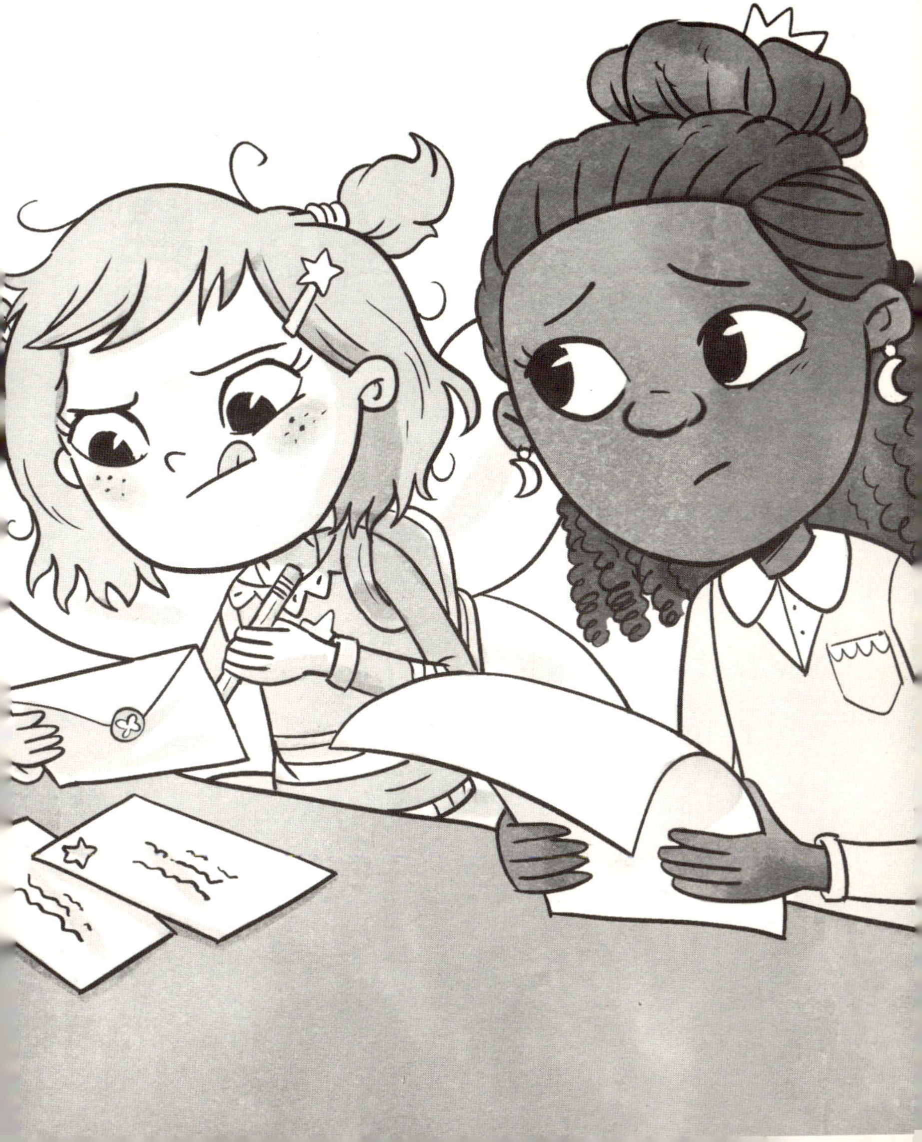

Chapter Two
Gifts from the Fairies

The day of the party had arrived and Verity was late. As she rushed out of her house, she saw Nissa.

"Are you late too?" asked Verity. She had completely forgotten that she hadn't invited Nissa. "Phew! I thought I would be the last fairy to arrive at the castle!"

"The castle?" replied Nissa. "What's happening at the castle?"

"The special party! To celebrate the arrival of Princess Rosamund. Everyone's going to be there."

"Everyone? I didn't know anything about a party!" frowned Nissa.

Verity gasped in horror as she realized what she'd done. But it was too late – Nissa had flown away in a **fury**.

*

When Verity arrived at the castle, her tummy felt funny. She tried to push away the memory of how upset Nissa had been. As she stepped inside, she admired the decorations she had organized. Peach, white, and silver balloons and big

fury   Very strong anger

gold-glittered banners filled the room. A **cascade** of magical sparkles floated from the ceiling down to the princess's cot. Butterfly-shaped lanterns twinkled on the huge banqueting table, which was full of food. In the middle of the room stood the most beautiful pink and white cake. It was made of marshmallows, and was in the shape of a castle. Verity was sure this was going to be the perfect party.

All the fairies had gathered around a grand four-poster cot. It was draped with white silk curtains. Inside was the cutest little baby with big brown eyes. All the fairies cooed over little Princess Rosamund as they presented their magic gifts to her.

---

cascade   Fall in huge amounts

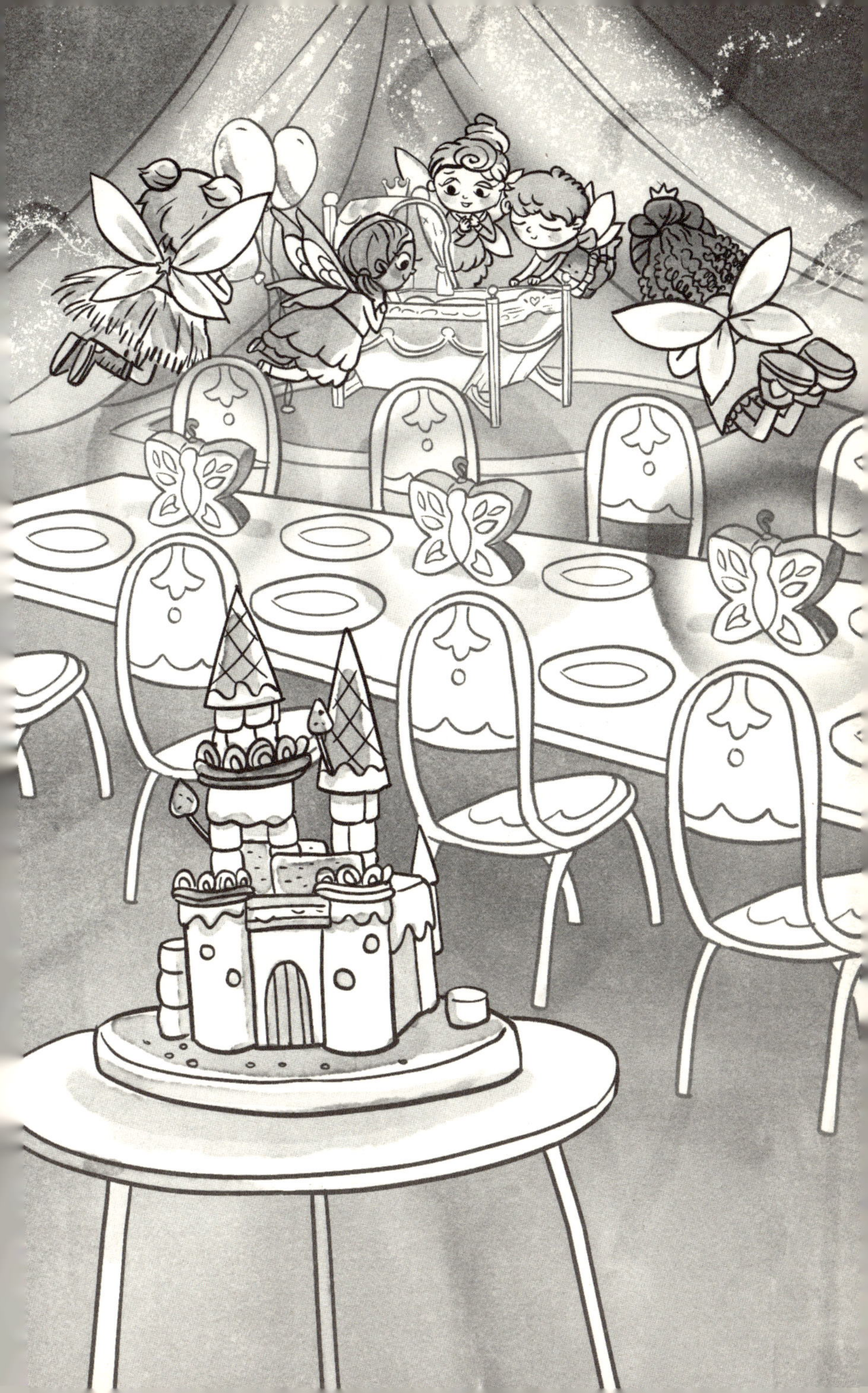

"What did you give?" whispered Verity to Celeste.

"I gave her the gift of wisdom," smiled Celeste.

"Oh, pickled pumpkins! I was going to give her that!" Verity tapped the side of her face with her finger. "Think, think, think," she said to herself. But she couldn't concentrate. All she could think of was how upset Nissa had been.

"What's wrong?" asked Celeste.

Verity shrugged. "I've just seen Nissa and she was very cross with me."

"Please tell me you didn't mention the party to her?" Celeste looked anxiously at Verity.

"I want to say I didn't mention it to her...

But… I can't… because… I might have mentioned it to her." Verity winced as she saw the look on Celeste's face.

But before Celeste could speak, the huge doors to the banqueting room flew open and there stood none other than, Nissa!

"Why am I the ONLY fairy not to have been invited?" Nissa was furious, her face red with anger.

The hall filled with fear. The deathly silence was broken by a tiny noise...

"Uh-oh!" squeaked Verity.

23

Chapter Three
Nissa's Curse

The King and Queen moved closer to welcome the angry fairy. "Maybe your invitation was lost in the post?" said the Queen nervously.

"I don't think so!" snarled Nissa. "Well, don't worry, I won't stay long. I just wanted to give Princess Rosamund my gift."

Nissa waved her wand over the cot.

"Princess Rosamund, you shall indeed dance gracefully, and be wise and happy. But one birthday, you shall prick your finger on a spinning wheel. Then you and everyone in the castle will fall down dead!" said Nissa nastily.

Everyone gasped. They couldn't believe Nissa would be so cruel.

Nissa slammed the huge wooden doors shut as she left.

"You can't fall down dead from pricking your finger with a wheel-thingy, can you?" Verity asked Celeste. Verity didn't know much about spinning wheels. But she knew Celeste loved doing cartwheels and she had never hurt herself.

"You shouldn't have left Nissa out. You need to put it right," Tatiana said firmly but kindly.

"How do I do that?" asked Verity.

"You're the only fairy not to have given your gift. You can't take away Nissa's awful **curse**, but you can make it better. Think carefully before you announce your gift and wave your wand." Tatiana smiled at Verity. "You can do this, Verity."

Verity felt proud that Tatiana believed in her. The only problem was, she really wasn't sure what to say.

"I keep thinking about what I would want if I were Princess Rosamund."

"That's good, Verity," Celeste said encouragingly. "What would that be?"

"Marshmallows!" Verity said dreamily.

Celeste placed her head in her hands.

curse   Magic spell to harm someone

Verity watched the King and Queen as they looked worriedly at their daughter and wept. She felt so sad for them all.

"I don't want them to die," sniffed Verity. "Why couldn't Nissa have said that Princess Rosamund will just 'sleep for a long time' instead?" She pulled a tissue out of Celeste's pocket, wiped her nose and put it back. "She's so mean!"

"That's it! Well done, Verity! You've just worked out a way to stop Nissa's spell!" Celeste said eagerly.

"I have?" Verity was **baffled**.

---

baffled   Confused and not understanding

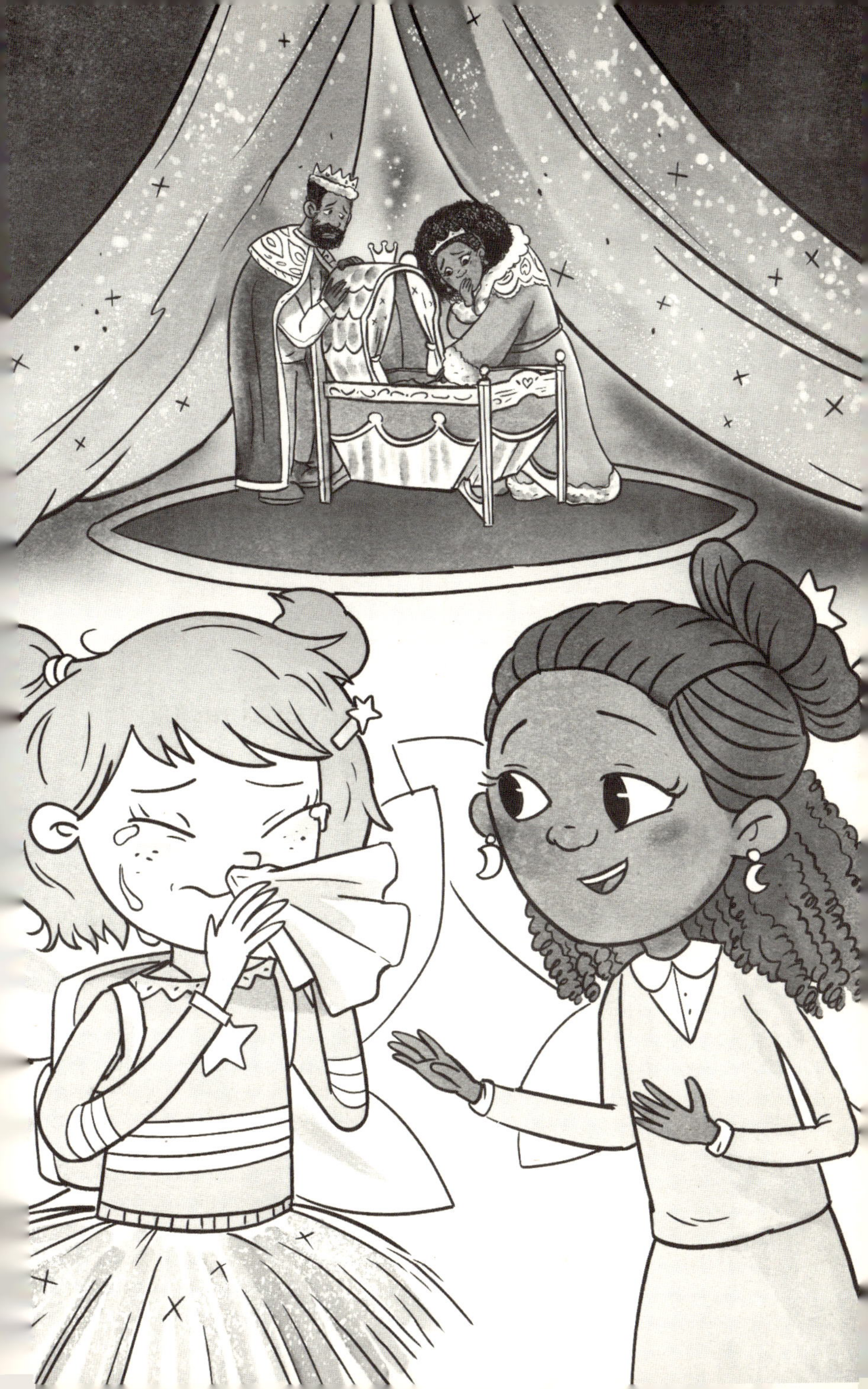

Chapter Four
A Marshmallow

Verity went over the words she had just said in her head. She thought for a few seconds and then she punched the air for joy. "I've got it!"

"I knew you could do it, Verity," Tatiana said happily. "Go ahead."

Verity cleared her throat. She felt very **nervous** as everyone stared at her. The King

---

30   **nervous**   Worried

and Queen held each other tightly as they waited for Verity to speak.

"Princess Rosamund, you shall indeed dance gracefully, and be wise and happy." Verity took a deep breath. "You will prick your finger BUT when you do, you and the whole castle will fall asleep and dream of marshmallows." Verity looked at the marshmallow in her hand and gleefully popped it into her mouth.

"Verity," whispered Tatiana. "You need to say how she will wake up!"

"Oh, yes, sorry," said Verity as she ate her marshmallow. "You will wake up when a prince..." Verity stopped and looked at Celeste, who was pointing at something.

"You've got a piece of marshmallow on your face," whispered Celeste.

Verity couldn't understand what Celeste was saying.

"Lick your face!" said Celeste, pointing to Verity's face.

"Licks your face?" repeated Verity.

A slow ripple of applause filled the room as everyone thought Verity had finished.

"Well done," said Tatiana, "you have saved the princess in your own unique way. With a prince who will... lick her face?" She shook her head as she walked away.

Verity beamed with relief.

"Wow!" exclaimed Celeste. "That was... great! But why does a prince have to lick her face to wake her up?"

"That's what you told me to say," said Verity **sternly**.

---

sternly   Seriously and strictly

Celeste frowned. "I was telling YOU to lick your face because you had a piece of marshmallow stuck to it. You looked a bit silly."

Verity felt very embarrassed.

"Thank you, Verity," interrupted the Queen. "As you have shown what a capable fairy you are, we would like you to be Princess Rosamund's fairy guardian."

Verity was shocked. "Thank you," she said proudly. "I won't let you down."

The King and Queen smiled happily as they left the fairies to enjoy the party.

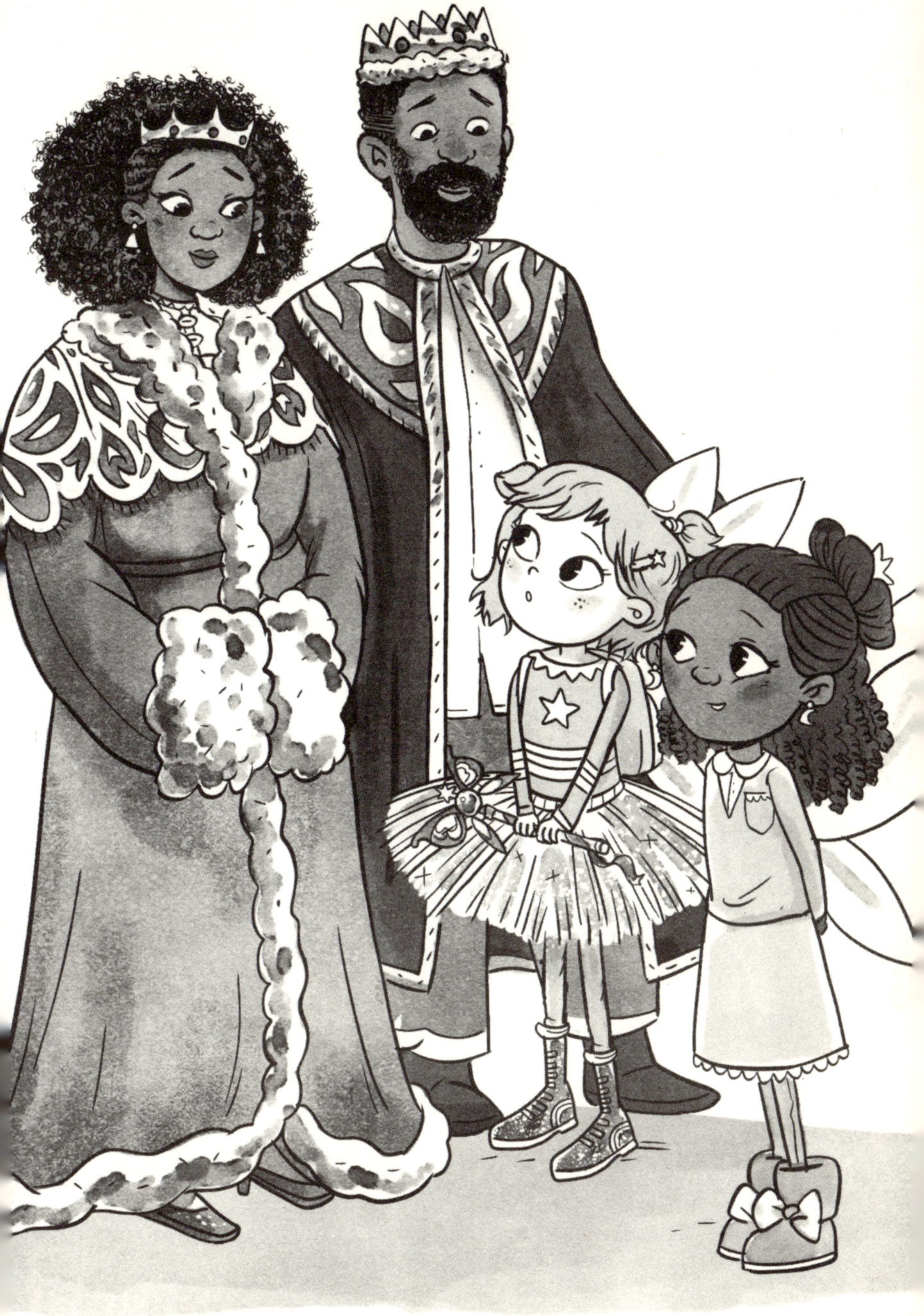

Chapter Five
A Fourth Birthday

Every time Princess Rosamund had a birthday, Verity was there to watch over her. Time is very different in the Fairy Tale Kingdom. Four years passed for the princess. But for Verity only four days had gone by and she was getting tired of birthdays!

Verity arrived in the castle grounds early

on Princess Rosamund's fourth birthday. She could hear her pretending to be an aeroplane.

"Where have you been? You're my passenger – run behind me," cried the princess as she raced past.

"I know, why don't we sit down and read a book?" Verity was keen to do something less energetic.

"But I'm an aeroplane!" replied the princess.

"Ooh, I know, we can play the piano! Or what about doing a jigsaw puzzle together?" Verity said breathlessly as she tried to catch up with the princess.

"I have a brilliant idea!" Princess Rosamund suddenly stopped running. She pulled off the netting of her skirt and threw it down on the grass. Underneath she was wearing her swimming costume over her tights. "I'm going to be a superhero!" she said. She held her arm straight up in front of her, ready to charge forward.

"I know what real superheroes like to do most," Verity said wide-eyed. "They like to sit down and read *Sparkle Time* while eating marshmallows." This was actually Verity's favourite thing to do.

Princess Rosamund screwed up her face. "No, they don't! They like to run around as fast as they can and chase the baddies." Verity could see the princess's bottom lip starting to wobble. She had to think of something else and quickly or the little princess would cry.

"Why don't we play... hide-and-seek?" suggested Verity.

"Yes! I'm really good at hiding! You count to one hundred and then come and find me. I bet you won't win!" called Princess Rosamund. As the princess ran inside the castle, Verity heard her whispering to herself, "Nobody ever goes in the room with the spinning wheel."

Verity shook her head. It was true nobody ever seemed to go in that room. She sat down on the grass and started counting.

When Verity finally reached one hundred she noticed that something was different. There was complete silence. No birds were singing, and the cooks weren't clattering pots and pans in the kitchen. It was as if the whole castle had fallen asleep. Verity suddenly remembered where Princess Rosamund had said she would hide. A tiny noise broke the silence.

"Uh-oh!" squeaked Verity.

Chapter Six
The Prince's Castle

Celeste flew to the castle to give her present to Princess Rosamund. As she arrived, she noticed how quiet it was. She spotted Verity sitting in the middle of the garden **sobbing**. Celeste put her arm around her friend.

Verity could just see Celeste through her tears. "It's... all... my... fault," she sniffed.

Celeste handed her a tissue.

---

sobbing   Crying uncontrollably

"I'm so silly!" Verity held her head in hands. "All I had to do was stop the princess going near a spinning wheel. I've let the King and Queen down and now Tatiana won't give me any important jobs and I'll never get a lilac sparkly star!"

"Verity, it's OK, because your gift is the

way to break Nissa's curse," Celeste reminded Verity. "You can do this. Everyone is counting on you."

Verity wiped the tears away from her eyes. "You're right, Celeste. I can do this! There's just one tiny problem."

"What's that?" asked Celeste.

"I need to find a prince who will lick Princess Rosamund's face!"

They both sighed.

"That's not going to be easy," Celeste frowned.

"Think, think, think. Where can we find a prince?" Verity said to herself.

Celeste grinned. "Prince Charming is holding one of his talks on 'how to be charming' at his palace. They're popular events and I'm sure we can find other princes there!"

Verity gasped. "I've always wanted to go to Prince Charming's palace." Verity tried to smooth down her pink hair. "Come on, what are we waiting for?"

Celeste chuckled. "I'd forgotten how much you like Prince Charming!"

The two fairies gently tucked the little princess, who was fast asleep, into her grand four-poster bed and set off for Prince Charming's castle.

When they arrived, they were amazed at how big it was. There were **turrets** on top of towered turrets and more windows than Verity could count. Sky-blue rooftops were edged with gold tiles and the light-pink stone of the castle made Verity's heart skip. She had never seen a building so beautiful.

"Wow! If this were a marshmallow cake I would eat it all up in one go!" sighed Verity happily.

"Let's knock on the door," said Celeste. She took Verity by the hand as they approached the huge wooden doors.

turrets Narrow towers

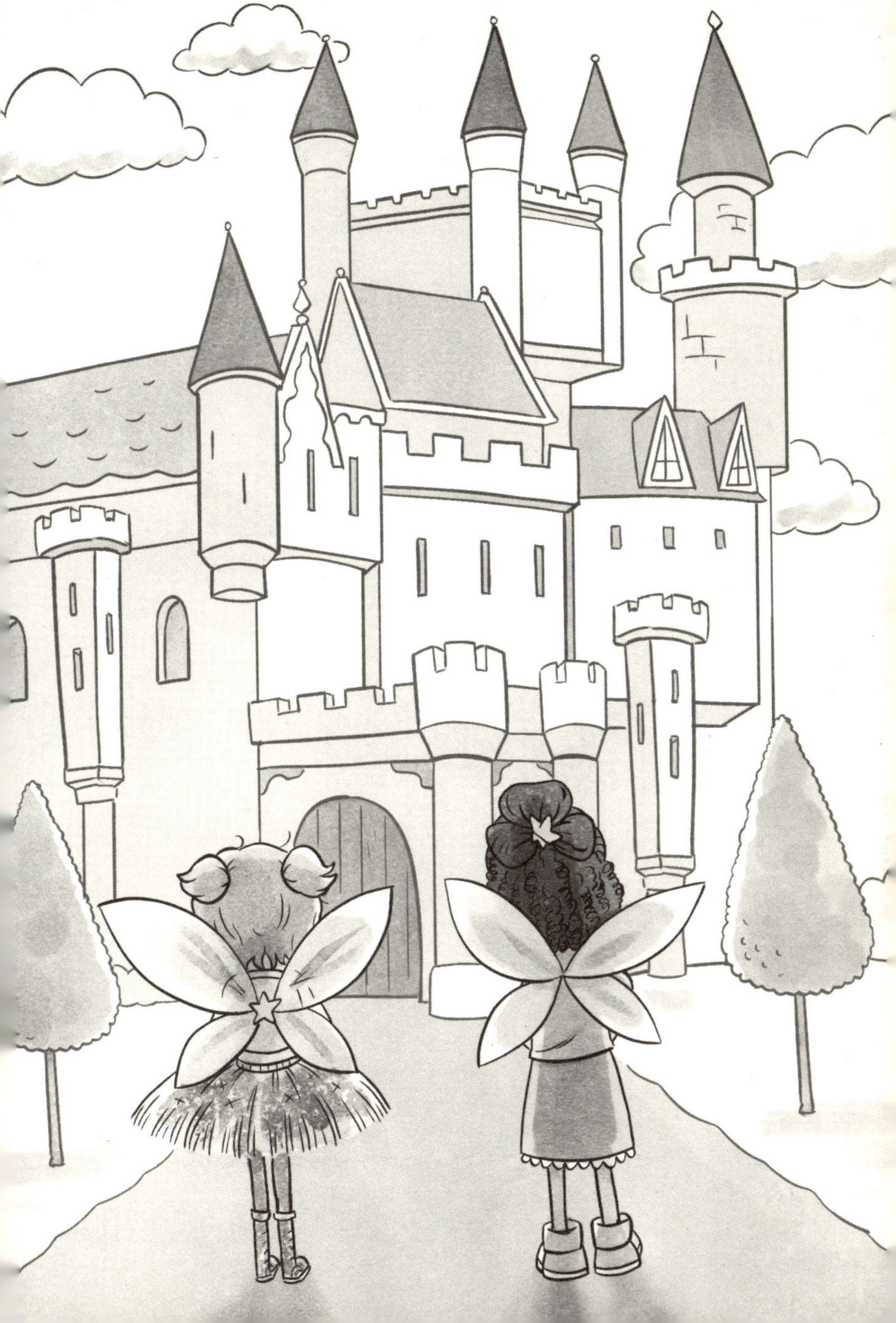

They nearly fell over when Prince Charming himself opened the door, but he ran straight past them followed by four other princes.

"Where are you going?" Verity shouted after them.

"To fight a dragon!" the last prince shouted back.

"Stop! Can you help us, please?" begged Verity.

But it was too late – the princes had gone.

Chapter Seven
Three Sparkly Stars

As they arrived back in the grounds of Sleeping Beauty's castle, the **silence was deafening**.

"I don't like this," Verity shuddered. "What are we going to do, Celeste? We need to find a prince to lick Princess Rosamund's face. If we don't, she may never wake up." Verity's dark-brown eyes started to fill with

---

silence was deafening   Easy-to-notice quietness

tears. "I'm really scared, Celeste," she sniffed.

Verity thought things couldn't get any worse. But then Nissa came bounding towards them with a white fluffy dog.

"Oh, pickled pumpkins! What is she doing here?" Verity stood up with her hands on her hips. "Nissa, if you've come here to be nasty again then you can leave RIGHT now!" Verity's voice was shaking with anger.

Nissa looked down at her bright-red sparkly boots. "I'm really sorry. I feel so bad for casting that nasty spell on Princess Rosamund. I've come here to try and make things better."

"Well, you're too late! The whole castle is in a deep sleep and we can't find a prince to lick Princess Rosamund's face. It's all your fault!" Verity folded her arms.

"I really am very sorry," sobbed Nissa. "How would you like it if you were the only fairy that hadn't been invited to the party?" Her sad green eyes filled with tears.

Verity and Celeste looked at each other.

Verity put her arm around Nissa. "You're right, Nissa. I'm sorry I didn't invite you to the party – it wasn't very nice of me. But what you did was very mean."

"I don't want to be mean. I just want to be included and have friends, like you." Nissa wiped her eyes.

"Me?" Verity had never thought Nissa would want to be like her. "But I thought you didn't like me. You were so very grumpy at my picnic! It really upset me, you know."

"I wasn't grumpy with you," sniffed Nissa. "I was grumpy because everybody had a dancing partner except me."

"I'm sorry, Nissa, I should have realized you were feeling left out." Verity gave Nissa a big hug.

"I'm glad we're friends again," beamed Nissa.

"But I still can't find a prince to wake Princess Rosamund." Verity felt very glum again.

Suddenly, Nissa clapped her hands together. "I've got it!" she announced gleefully. "Verity, take this." She handed Verity the dog's lead.

Verity frowned as the dog jumped up excitedly.

"Look at his collar," Nissa told Verity.

"Um, yes, it's a very nice shade of blue." Verity was confused. It looked just like any other dog collar.

"His name is on the collar." Nissa pointed to the silver pendant.

Verity read it. "Pickled pumpkins!" she gasped. "Celeste, look at this!"

"Prince!" read Celeste, as she raised an eyebrow at Verity.

The three fairies took Prince, the dog, to

where Princess Rosamund was still sound asleep.

"How do you make a dog lick your face?" said Celeste as she tried to think of a way. But the furry little dog had already jumped onto Princess Rosamund's bed and was enthusiastically licking the little girl's face.

"That tickles!" giggled Princess Rosamund as she opened her eyes and sat up. "Ah, he's such a cute dog. Can I keep him? Please, please, please?"

In the castle all around them, people started stretching and yawning as they woke up.

Verity was so delighted, she jumped up and down. "We did it!" she squealed as she hugged Celeste and Nissa. The three fairies danced around in a circle.

Princess Rosamund ran around the garden chasing Prince, who barked joyfully. They both looked so happy playing together.

*

The next evening, all the fairies gathered around the enchanted tree. The full moon glowed brightly above them. Verity, Celeste, and Nissa chatted excitedly. Then a **hush** fell as Tatiana began to speak.

"Usually, I only award one special star. But tonight I am very happy to be awarding THREE." Tatiana's eyes shone. She motioned for Verity, Celeste, and Nissa to come forward. "These three fairies saved Princess Rosamund. But they also helped and cared

---

hush   Quiet and peaceful moment

for each other. They showed us the true meaning of friendship. I'm so very proud of you all for working so well together."

The three fairies each opened their magical box. Celeste's sparkly blue star floated high in the sky and then came back down to land in her hands. Then came Nissa's sparkly red star, and Verity's shiny pink star.

All the fairies clapped and cheered.

Celeste could tell that Verity was a little disappointed. She knew her friend had really wanted a lilac star.

Tatiana handed another box to Verity. "This gift is for you from the King and Queen. It's a special thank you for looking after the princess."

Verity was thrilled. As she lifted the lid and looked inside, she gasped loudly.

"Do you like it?" Celeste asked, bouncing on her toes.

"It's amazing!" Verity lifted out an

amazing marshmallow cake. It was in the shape of Prince Charming's castle.

All the fairies gathered around Verity. They had never seen a cake so beautiful.

"Don't worry, I'll share this with everyone. After all, you are ALL my friends." Verity smiled at Nissa. "I get the biggest piece though." Verity licked her lips.

Nissa chuckled. "You're one of a kind, Verity!"

Fairy Quiz

1. Which fairy did Verity not invite to the party?

2. What gift did Celeste give the baby princess at her party?

3. Which game did Verity play with Princess Rosamund on her fourth birthday?

4. Where were Prince Charming and the four princes going when they rushed past Verity and Celeste?

5. What colour are Nissa's sparkly boots?

6. What is the name of the dog that licked Princess Rosamund's face?

7. Why was Nissa grumpy at Verity's picnic?

8. What was Verity's gift from the King and Queen at the end?

Answers

1. Nissa 2. Wisdom 3. Hide-and-seek 4. To fight a dragon 5. Red 6. Prince 7. She didn't have a dancing partner 8. A marshmallow cake

Illustrations by Amy Zhing
Designed by Collaborate Agency
Fiction editor Heather Featherstone
Educational consultants Jacqueline Harris, Jenny Lane-Smith

Senior editors Amy Braddon, Marie Greenwood
Senior designer Ann Cannings
Managing editor Laura Gilbert
Managing art editor Diane Peyton Jones
Production editor Dragana Puvacic
Production controller Francesca Sturiale
Publishing manager Francesca Young

First published in Great Britain in 2021 by
Dorling Kindersley Limited
DK, One Embassy Gardens, 8 Viaduct Gardens,
London, SW11 7BW

The authorised representative in the EEA is
Dorling Kindersley Verlag GmbH. Arnulfstr. 124,
80636 Munich, Germany

Copyright © 2021 Dorling Kindersley Limited
A Penguin Random House Company
10 9 8 7 6 5 4 3 2 1
001–323741–Nov/2021

All rights reserved.
No part of this publication may be reproduced, stored in or introduced into a retrieval system, or transmitted, in any form, or by any means (electronic, mechanical, photocopying, recording, or otherwise), without the prior written permission of the copyright owner.

A CIP catalogue record for this book
is available from the British Library.
ISBN: 9-780-2415-0346-1

Printed and bound in Great Britain by
Clays Ltd, Elcograf S.p.A.

For the curious
www.dk.com

MIX
Paper from
responsible sources
FSC™ C018179

This book was made with Forest Stewardship Council™ certified paper – one small step in DK's commitment to a sustainable future. For more information go to www.dk.com/our-green-pledge